Wag Your Tail

Wag Your Tail

Dog Stories
and
Poems to Touch Your Heart

POETSENVY

iUniverse, Inc.
Bloomington

Wag Your Tail
Dog Stories and Poems to Touch Your Heart

iUniverse books may be ordered through booksellers or by contacting:

iUniverse
1663 Liberty Drive
Bloomington, IN 47403
www.iuniverse.com
1-800-Authors (1-800-288-4677)

ISBN: 978-1-4759-8813-0 (sc)
ISBN: 978-1-4759-8814-7 (ebk)

Library of Congress Control Number: 2013907656

Printed in the United States of America

iUniverse rev. date: 04/24/2013

Contents

Dedication

From the moment we enter this world we are searching for love and companionship. I was fortunate to be born into a family in which love was abundant, and I was allowed to explore the world on my own terms. My parents loved and educated me; my brothers and sisters taught me the world was friendly and exciting; and dogs, my furry friends, helped keep me safe and content.

This book contains stories and poems about dogs. From my early childhood until the present time, dogs have impacted and changed how I've related to my human friends. From dogs I've learned that loyalty, unconditional love, vulnerability, discipline, consistency, and teamwork are all important. Learning their rules eased my way into the world of humans.

Perhaps dogs understand much more than we give them credit for. Right away they decide whether a newcomer is a friend or a foe to be reckoned with. A friend is a friend for life. A friend's scent is never forgotten even though eyesight or hearing fails. A foe is equally remembered until proven otherwise.

In this collection of short stories and poems dogs live and die, interact with the world, and become members of my family and yours. If these stories touch your heart or remind you of your childhood, then I have succeeded. If you are entertained and distracted from the world's problems, then share the stories with others. Dogs and their stories are one way of bringing love and companionship into the world.

I have learned approaches to life from dogs. If I want to get along with others in the world, I don't have to wag my tail, but it does help to smile.

The first five stories in this collection of dog stories are about Belle, a Lhasa Apso. Lhasa Apsos, one of the oldest dog breeds in the world, are highly respected for their keen sense of hearing. Belle's ancestors were originally used to alert Buddhist monks to intruders who entered the monasteries.

In this story Belle was caught off guard and did not warn her owner about a burglar. However, she saved the day by finding a way to overcome her mistake.

Belle Has to Lead!

The big dogs could have eaten Belle in one mighty gulp.
She was fearless, so she let them rough her up.
Often she romped happily with her canine friends.
When life is good like that, the fun never ends.

To other dogs, her personality was like a soothing balm.
This Tibetan bearded lion dog always remained calm.
Playing with others became part of her daily game.
But Belle would stop her play when she heard me call her name.

Her best friend, though, was Fluffy the Cat.
She would chase him, and they would wrestle on the mat.
They played day and night until they finally went to sleep.
Exhausted, they would snuggle together in a little heap.

One evening before dinner I was watching a show.
An intruder entered; it was someone I didn't know.
He carried a gun, and I had no time to react.
As he tied me up, Belle hid, but then she came back.

With derision, the stranger said, "If that dog is so wise,
How did I get the jump on you guys?"
He lit a cigarette and leaned against a wall.
"You're all tied up, and there's no one to help at all."

He smiled smugly and snarled, "If you make one sound,
You and that worthless dog are going down."
Belle distracted him as she dashed from room to room.
The burglar opened the back door, and out the door she zoomed.

The burglar called out to his pals, "Hey, watch out for the men in blue.
If I find you slacking, then I'll be all over you."
His two lookouts grunted. "We're on it. We've got it covered far and wide."
The burglar felt he had control, so he came back inside.

At top speed, Belle raced around corners and bends.
Then silent shapes joined her to help save her friend.
She led three Dobermans in a blitz the lookouts did not detect.
The lookouts were knocked to the ground; the attack they did not expect.

Without a bark between them, the big dogs knew what to do.
They stayed while the little dog continued onward, leading a motley crew.
There were Chihuahuas, terriers, bassets, and two Rottweilers on the run.
Not a single dog was willing to miss out on the evening's fun.

The burglar heard a slew of sounds, ranging from a squeak to a roar.
While he grinned at the sight, one dog slipped through the door.
On the top of the couch Belle found her viewing place.
The burglar took aim and shouted, "Get out of my face!"

At that moment Fluffy jumped on the burglar's head.
The burglar shrieked as the cat took care of him instead.
Belle laughed to see such sport as the burglar thrashed around.
Both Rottweilers pounced on him and made sure he stayed down.

A patrol car pulled up, and two policemen got out.
They were met by a Lhasa Apso that continued to race about.
She led them to the place where two men lay on the ground.
One of the policemen said, "Well, look at what we've found."

"Roll over," the other policeman ordered. "Keep your hands behind
   your back.
Don't move. I don't want these dogs to attack."
One officer stayed while the other followed Belle into the house.
Outside, dogs were running everywhere. Inside it was quiet as a
   mouse.

The burglar lay on the floor, watched by dogs and cat.
His face was scratched, and his pants were torn right where he sat.
"Please, Officer, I can't move around, and I can't see.
If I turn just one little bit, these animals might attack me.

"Take me in and put me in a safe cell.
I have my rights, and I know them well.
I'll sue that man for all that he's done.
He's the only one here, so he must be the guilty one."

I laughed. "I'm still tied up. You tied the knots well.
Think about that while you're sitting in your cell."
He stared at me oddly, which drew the cat's hiss.
I said, "You'd better be careful glaring at me like this."

More officers arrived and put the bad guys in patrol cars.
The burglar was crying because he thought he might have scars.
A detective approached me with a pen in his hand.
"I have questions to ask. There are things I don't understand."

"Who got all the dogs involved? And what about the cat?
How did you do all this, tied up like that?
The three perpetrators are as confused as anyone.
Oh, one more question. Who called 9-1-1?"

When the officers drove away and I was left alone,
I patted each dog and the cat and hung up the phone.
"Belle, you did well rounding up your friends.
But you had too much fun. Wipe off your grin."

I gave the animals treats and sent them all home.
"Come back and visit if you need somewhere to roam."
Wearily I climbed into bed and turned out the light.
I thought about the events that had transpired on this interesting
    night.

Following directions is considered a sign of dogs being smart.
But Belle showed her intelligence by knowing where to start.
Other dogs might appear to be smarter, so I'm teaching her to read.
But Belle already knows they have to follow and she has to lead.

Greet each day with enthusiasm and be willing to try new things.

Belle loved riding in cars and putting her head out the window. She loved diving in and thrashing about in a swimming pool. She had even considered going on a roller coaster. But skydiving? That was beyond her comfort level.

Belle Goes Skydiving

I told Belle about the skydiving trip, but I don't think she liked the idea. Loud noises frightened her, and she was also afraid of heights. Why would she want to leave the ground and jump from an airplane? It didn't make sense. She liked being safe and secure. Skydiving had to be dangerous. The only thing that might change her mind was watching me have fun. She didn't like to be left out of anything I seemed to enjoy. If she waited for a few minutes, I was sure she would join right in.

Although Belle was hesitant to try new experiences, she hated being left home alone even more. She probably thought she could go along for the ride and watch me jump. But she was wrong. After we climbed aboard the plane, I immediately strapped her tightly against my chest. There was no doubt we would jump together. I could feel her heart pounding as the plane taxied down the runway and lifted off.

The roar of the plane's engines scared her, but she did not struggle to get away. She trusted me. I was sure she could endure the noise and vibrations for a little while. When I got up and walked to the door, I noticed her eyes were closed.

Suddenly I jumped out and away from the plane. As we fell toward the earth, the air rushed against us. Belle shook her head and relaxed. She didn't seem afraid. This must have felt much like riding in a car with her head out of the window.

At first nothing was recognizable as we plunged downward. Then a multicolored patchwork of farms stretched out before us. The diverse scene changed into shapes that became familiar as rivers, roads, and trees grew larger.

I pulled the cord and felt a sharp tug. The parachute opened and stretched out, full of air. For her, it must have been like someone pulling her leash. I guided the parachute in large circles as we descended. A wind gust carried me away from my chosen landing spot, but I noticed a freshly plowed field nearby. We drifted downward, aiming for that field. We hit the ground harder than I expected, and I tumbled several times before coming to a stop. I hurried to get untangled because Belle didn't seem to be moving.

After I slipped out of the harness, I checked on Belle. I think she enjoyed the rough landing because she appeared to be unhurt— smiling and eager to be free of the tight straps. Belle waited patiently while I gathered our equipment.

Our ride arrived shortly after, and my friend drove us back to the airport, where I retrieved my car. "Thanks for picking us up," I said, "especially since we drifted off course."

"How was your experience with your dog? Did she like the jump?"

"Being partnered with Belle made the experience more interesting, and she did even better than I expected."

When we arrived home, Belle seemed to look at things with a new perspective. I think Belle changed her mind about surprises, and if she had known we were going to have fun skydiving, she would not have hidden under the bed. Instead, she had another experience to share with her friends.

Now that she had experienced that new adventure, she eagerly awaited the next one. Whenever she saw me packing my suitcase, she stayed by my side, her brown eyes pleading, *Take me! Take me!*

I never want to be afraid of learning, even when it might hurt.

Therapy dogs come in all sizes and breeds. They work in hospitals, in assisted living homes, and in schools with children who have learning difficulties. The dogs must be friendly, patient, confident, gentle, and at ease in all situations. They have to maintain their composure around unfamiliar people or unfamiliar equipment.

There are reports that interactions with therapy dogs can increase oxytocin (bonding) and dopamine (happiness) while lowering cortisol (stress). Belle used her training as a therapy dog to defuse an explosive situation and make friends at the same time.

Belle Goes to School
and Becomes a Therapy Dog

One Sunday as I finished giving Belle her weekly scrub,
Her expression said, *I'm tired of being in the tub*.
She looked shaggy while wet, and she still needed a trim.
I don't think she cared much for her little swim.

As soon as her feet hit the bathroom floor,
She dashed lickety-split out the bathroom door.
Vigorously she shook and gave a final shrug.
She began racing from room to room and then rug to rug.

I pretended to chase her, and I really did try.
Her energy seemed endless, and she needed to dry.
Like a clock with a spring, she finally wound down.
She lay there for a moment and didn't make a sound.

I thought she said, *"I've been watching the kids go to school.
I'm ready to go too. It looks pretty cool."*
I drove to school with Belle in the back.
She knew she would have to stay quiet in my backpack.

Even for a teacher, dogs weren't usually allowed at school.
But Belle looked so happy, I was willing to stretch the rule.
The morning went smoothly. You might say it was a breeze.
Belle took her constitutional after a lunch of mac and cheese.

My lessons were great, but they might have been boring.
As the afternoon progressed, I heard Belle snoring.
If everyone stayed quiet, that was okay with me,
But a rascal named Joe had an insatiable curiosity.

He was fidgety, talkative, and could not sit still.
He teased the girls relentlessly and gave them a thrill.
Wanting to impress the girls with how tough he could be,
It was evident he was ready to challenge anyone. Even me!

Belle was restless. I think she could sense that trouble was ready to
    brew.
She jumped out of the backpack. She knew what to do.
Joe's admirers saw Belle and left him behind.
Without an audience, he nearly lost his mind.

Joe was ready to fight everyone he could see.
Of course his first target happened to be me.
Belle was aware that Joe didn't care at all.
That's when she brought him his favorite thing: a soccer ball.

My class went outside to witness the ultimate game.
It was Joe and his friends against me and what's-her-name.
It was hard fought, and Joe did his best.
The score was tied near the end of the contest.

Belle looked at Joe and then gave me a grin.
She sealed their friendship when she let him win.
The principal arrived and demanded, "Why is this dog here?"
Joe answered boldly, "She's our therapy dog this year!"

From then on when Belle was at school,
Joe claimed he taught her to read because she was so cool.
She knew not to argue when she had it so good,
Because Belle, the therapy dog, always understood.

When action is needed, I want to be there to help—not yesterday, not tomorrow, but now.

There are some people who try to take away joy and happiness. Those are people to growl at.

Belle used her own version of the Heimlich maneuver when she prevented a girl from choking on a piece of food. Belle's emergency technique saved Suzi's life.

Belle Uses the Heimlich Maneuver

Belle accompanied me during my first aid course renewal. I read the book, took and passed the tests, and received my certification. I was prepared for emergencies at school. Belle, on the other hand, slept through the process. In my opinion she had learned nothing.

The next Friday, the school cafeteria was nosier than usual. A special program had been introduced, and everyone was excited. The elementary classes had listened and watched as a salesman explained how easy it was to win prizes and raise funds for the school just by selling cookie dough. And if they sold cookie dough on the very first day, they could win money and candy prizes.

This was a win-win-win situation. Students competed to be heard as plans were made and strategies mapped out. The upcoming weekend was the start of the campaign, and everybody wanted to win prizes.

Joe was especially excited. Although Joe was normally talkative and restless, today he was serious and quiet. He stood out in a sea of faces as he contemplated how to win without stirring up problems. He knew a lot of places where he could sell cookie dough. That wasn't the real challenge. He wanted to win and prove he was a better salesman than Scott. Scott was his archenemy and a bully. Scott also wanted to win, and he didn't want any competition. He had already warned Joe not to try so hard.

Belle, in her therapy role, was bored with all the talk, and no one was paying any attention to her. Her senses were working overtime. The cafeteria food, hotdogs and beans, didn't smell as good as she had hoped. She decided to wait for something better.

She lay near Joe's feet, listening intently to the children's excited chatter. Something did not sound right. In the middle of the uproar there was a sudden change. One of the loudest voices ceased.

Acting on a hunch, Belle raced to the place where the loud voice had diminished into dreadful silence. A girl was turning purple. With her hands at her throat, she made no sound, but her eyes and expression desperately pleaded for help.

Without wondering whether she had read about this or had seen this happen, Belle hurled herself against the girl's back. *Whack!* A piece of hotdog popped from the girl's mouth. The girl gasped for breath as she slowly returned to normal.

Scott yelled, "This dog just attacked without warning! I knew this dog was dangerous."

Joe sputtered, "Belle saved Suzi's life. If Belle hadn't hit Suzi's back, then she might have choked to death."

Scott ranted, "Belle attacked her. I was the one who saved her from choking." He pointed at a second grader. "What did you see?" he demanded.

"Just what you said. The dog jumped on her."

Scott looked at the principal. "That dog attacked Suzi, but I saved her life. I should get some recognition, and that dog needs to be out."

Belle didn't want praise for herself. She just wanted Suzi to be okay and everything back to normal. She knew Scott was lying, but how could she prove him wrong? And did it really matter?

Suzi painfully rasped, "Belle saved my life! Scott was laughing at me because I was choking. He didn't help. It was the dog that saved me."

Other voices chimed in. Nobody had been willing to go against Scott until Suzi spoke up. There seemed to be safety in numbers, and now they all clamored to be heard. Scott turned to Joe. "I'll get you for this," he vowed. "You and that dumb dog!"

He stomped off, angry at Belle, angry at Joe, and angry at the world.

Joe was more serious than ever about winning the cookie dough contest. He didn't want to worry about Scott and his threats. Scott might try to beat him up, but Joe wasn't afraid. He would stand up to Scott next time. Bullies only got worse if they got their way.

I let my heart guide my day and help those who come my way.

Belle's senses were often put to test. I had to learn to trust her instincts, wherever she might lead.

In the following story, no Amber Alert had been issued, but Belle knew something was wrong. She was alert and ready, expectantly waiting to help whoever needed her.

Belle Rides Shotgun!
(AMBER Alert)

She rode in the car with the wind in her face.
The passenger side was her favorite place.
When Belle pushed the button, she always knew
She'd have the wind, the front seat, and a great view.

It takes more than the wind to make her grin.
An open window is a place for her to begin.
She sees the world as she thinks it should be.
It's nicer when everyone is happy; don't you agree?

Belle and I were going shopping one afternoon.
It was one of those hot sunny days in late June.
She rode with her head out the window to enjoy the air.
The temperature was still rising, but she didn't care.

"Belle," I said, "dogs aren't allowed inside the mall.
We'll get an ice cream cone and then go. That's all."
If one food is her favorite, it might be ice cream.
I expected Belle to be excited, maybe even scream.

She struggled and fought to be on the ground.
Her expression had changed; now she wore a frown.
The pavement was burning her little paws,
But she was in rescue mode, and she had an important cause.

She dashed three rows away to a car that was shut tight.
The car appeared to be empty. No one was in sight.
Belle was insistent. She refused to leave.
She was giving me a message that I chose to believe.

As I got closer, I found to my surprise
That children were inside. I saw two sets of eyes.
Their faces were flushed. Their condition was poor.
I had no time to think. I tugged hard at the door.

The door was locked, and the children looked afraid.
How could I get them out and into the cool shade?
I called 9-1-1 and waited for their parents to show.
Should I break a window? I didn't quite know.

Belle was running in large circles, but she didn't travel far.
She heard a siren and led firemen to the car.
The children were rescued, but Belle still refused to go.
She wanted to show me something I didn't yet know.

I listened intently after I opened the car door.
Tightly wrapped in a blanket, a baby lay on the car floor.
Before I could call for help, a fireman was at my side.
He had seen me follow Belle. His eyes were open wide.

The firemen's procedures were smooth and quickly carried out.
The two children recovered quickly. The baby's life was still in
    doubt.
Belle watched closely and then walked away.
I could tell by her demeanor the baby would be okay.

"We'd like to take Belle with us," was one fireman's remark.
"She had so much to tell us without even one frantic bark.
She was calm in an emergency, and she was constantly aware.
A dog that can do so many things is certainly very rare."

A woman began to scream and cry, "What have you done to my car?
You've broken a window, and my house is so far!
My children don't like the air blowing in their faces.
Somebody has to repair this window. We still have to go places."

Belle growled at the woman, informing me something was not right.
Belle rarely growled, but this time she was ready to fight.
The children clung to my legs and got behind me.
I wanted to ask Belle, "What could the problem be?"

"Don't worry, ma'am. Whenever there's some doubt,
We call the sheriff, and he can work it all out."
The fireman wanted to move the kids away from any harm.
The woman's actions were suspicious and caused us alarm.

"Come on, kids," she said with a worried frown.
But she ignored the baby, who still lay on the ground.
Belle blocked her path so the woman couldn't escape.
I thought, *All Belle needs now is a Superman's cape.*

Several police cars arrived at nearly the same time.
Apparently the police had been working nearby on a major crime.
They surrounded the woman, and no one was hurt.
One deputy said, "You must have heard about the AMBER Alert!"

But Belle didn't like all the publicity or strife.
All she wanted to do was live a quiet life.
No matter how exciting life was each day,
She wanted to relax and then eat and go play.

Belle had earned the right to do as she pleased,
Like riding up front with her face in the breeze.
Even with all of her quirks, Belle stayed focused and alert.
She never wanted to see children get hurt.

When all was explained from the beginning to the end,
All were convinced that Belle had a reason to grin.
She had helped capture a woman who was committing a crime.
Most importantly, she found the children while there was still time.

Belle is not always aware of her surroundings. Sometimes when she hides from me, she forgets to pull her tail under the bed. She's very quiet, but that tail is a definite indication that she is there. I pretend not to see her tail, and I call for her. When I go into another room, she will suddenly appear, pleased that I couldn't find her.

Sometimes I have to stand up for what I believe is true and trust my own senses!

Your Pets Know

When you're alone or scared at night and feeling very tense,
Who knows what dogs hear, and who knows what they sense?
A dog might snarl and show her teeth while staring at a wall;
Something might have entered the room, yet you see nothing at all.
When the silence gets too loud during the time that you fear most,
You'll wish you had a dog around to warn you of the ghosts.
A faint smell of decaying flesh or a chill running up your spine
Is enough to put your teeth on edge, but when the dog starts to
    whine,
A powerful force is in the room, sharing your time and space.
Your dog will remain beside you as the demon meets you
    face-to-face.
A cat, on the other hand, might hiss and arch his back.
A cat knows whether the force is friend or foe and if the demon will
    attack.
Should the cat stretch and purr as if stroked by a ghostly hand,
There's a gentle soul in the room who hopes you understand.
If either the dog or the cat runs, terror evident in their eyes,
Then it might not be a simple ghost but the devil in disguise.
Pull the covers over your head should you be scared at night,
But if you want a chance to flee, keep your pets in plain sight.

Something's Out There!

Although they were from the same litter, my two black Labrador retrievers were definitely different. Roxy was sleek and feminine, obedient, and quiet. Pixie, also a female, was tough, rough, and independent. Despite their differences the dogs worked in unison, complementing each other's personalities.

Because of their calm demeanors and gentle dispositions, people often overlooked them. They were obedience trained. It was rare for either dog to bark or whine. They never demanded anything or questioned. They usually waited patiently until I was ready to listen. Sometimes, though, they were persistent until I realized the importance of their message.

One particular evening they had been up and down, and their restlessness was getting on my nerves. "Would you stop it?" I said loudly to them. I commanded them to lie down, and they looked at me questioningly as if I was making a mistake. After a short time, both got up and walked to the front door, bumped the doorknob, and stared at me. I was too busy to pay much attention because I was trying to finish a poem on the computer.

Their behavior grew worse. Now they bumped the knob and softly growled. *They're acting very strangely,* I thought, but I continued on with my work. Finally they plopped down next to me and stared at the door.

Usually they were very well behaved and obedient. A month before, I had taken them with me to a family reunion in Colorado. They had stayed out of trouble, played with the young children, caught two mice in my cabin, and performed flawlessly at a talent show as they went through their repertoire of tricks. They not only executed the basic commands but remembered all of their more advanced tricks. They had been stars and were invited back.

I expected their good behavior at all times, and sometimes that obedience brought unexpected results. For example, the week before, they had been wearing harnesses and lying in the bed of my truck. They were so quiet that I had forgotten they were there.

In the meantime, my basset hound, Scooter, had wandered into the road, following some long-lost scent. Scooter had very little training and had a tendency to do what she wanted. I was determined to change Scooter's freewheeling behavior to obedience.

"Scooter!" I had commanded sternly. "Come!" She had continued down the road with her nose to the ground, oblivious to my command. "Scooter!" I shouted. "Come!"

Scooter had paid no attention, but the two Labs had leaped into action. Both had jumped over the tailgate when they heard my command. Now they dangled over the tailgate, suspended in midair, hanging by their harnesses, unhurt but looking foolish. I had felt even more foolish because I had given a command in their presence, and they had just tried to please me.

Now as I watched them pacing the floor, I could tell they were distracted by something outside. "Okay," I said. "Let's go and see what's there."

Roxy raced in front of me and blocked my path to the door. "You're so funny, Roxy," I said. "Now get out of the way. I want to go outside."

Both brushed past me and began sniffing the air, the ground, and then one of the nearby trees. Pixie began throwing herself high against the tree, trying to catch a branch. Roxy also began leaping into the air, making strange high-pitched yelps. I could see nothing in the darkness. The dogs were still leaping and trying to climb the tree nearest me. Finally I turned back to the house. "Come on. There's nothing out here. You're making a big fuss over nothing." Once inside they quieted right down.

Two days later I was talking to one of my friends about how deer hunting had lost its excitement. "Not for me," he interrupted. "Wait a minute. I've got a picture I want to show you. I took it two days ago, not far from here."

He went to his truck and returned in a few moments. "I was alone when I shot a buck. I wanted to take my picture with it to show my friends. I put my camera on a tripod, set the timer, and posed. I didn't realize what a good picture it was until I brought the camera to a photo shop to have copies made. Take a good look at the picture and tell me what you think."

This was ridiculous, I thought. I'd seen enough hunters posing with a freshly killed deer. But to humor my friend, I took the photograph and looked it over. The camera's flash clearly showed him kneeling proudly by his deer. I started to put the photo down when I noticed a large tawny shape advancing toward him. A mountain lion was behind him and had been within ten feet when the flash went off.

Startled, I looked up questioningly. "Is this for real?"

"Yes," he said. "The cougar was probably after the deer I was holding, but I don't know for sure. I think the flash happened at the right second and scared the cougar away. I didn't know cougars were in this area until I got the pictures. I reported the incident to the game warden, but he was skeptical. Have you noticed anything strange around here?"

"No, not at all," I replied. I had forgotten about the dogs' strange behavior.

A few days later while thumbing through the local paper, I glanced at a small article that showed a picture of a mountain lion on a branch. According to the article, hunters had spotted the mountain lion while hunting in southern Platte County. Experts from the state fish and game agency verified the mountain lion's presence by hair and scratch marks. They said the cougar had wandered far outside its natural boundaries because of the shrinking deer population.

Now I was really curious about Roxy and Pixie's behavior. I went outside and looked up at the tree. Just above the first large branch were several scratches and clumps of tawny hair. Shivers went up and down my spine.

"When will I ever learn to listen to those dogs?" I asked myself as I went inside. "I'm just not as smart as I think I am sometimes. Something was out there!"

Along with all of life's questions, there are answers hidden close by. I'll try to use all my senses and develop my hunches.

Chasing Rabbits

It could be my imagination, but I think rabbits trick me. I can understand that. But the rabbits also found ways to confuse the Labs.

Sometimes I would take my two Labs, Roxy and Pixie, down to the river for long walks and let them explore. Not only did it offer a change of scenery, but it gave me time to reflect about life in general. During one of those outings, I observed how my life worked and why I never seemed to get ahead. After watching the dogs in their endeavors, I decided that, like my dogs, I've always chased rabbits.

Roxy was the faster of the two dogs and also the more skilled hunter. She made wide sweeps through the brush and flushed out rabbits that were hiding there. Pixie ran ahead and waited for the rabbits to be driven her way.

The rabbits would jump out of the brush and race for shelter, always with Roxy in hot pursuit. Pixie would be ready, but somehow the rabbits would outmaneuver or jump at just the right time and escape. I didn't pay much attention at first, but soon I noticed that the results were the same each and every time.

I set up an observation point so I could watch an entire chase. Although the chase went smoothly, Roxy and Pixie's efforts proved fruitless. Somehow, though, I had a hunch that deception was taking place right before my eyes and that I was missing a key ingredient of the action. I needed more information to formulate a reasonable explanation.

Seeking to solve the mystery, I brought my camcorder, set up a folding chair in the shade of a large oak tree, and got ready for action.

It did not take long before Roxy flushed out a rabbit. It ran as expected, increasing its lead for a moment. As Roxy gained and drew closer, Pixie waited and dashed in just as the rabbit came into view. The rabbit seemed to find a sudden burst of energy and got away. At least it seemed that way as I watched in real time.

Later, as I reviewed the movie I had taken of the chase, I noticed a few strange details. The rabbit getting away at the end was not the same rabbit at the beginning of the chase. After studying the movie in slow motion, I came to the conclusion that there were four rabbits, and they seemed to be in a relay. The first rabbit got a big lead, slowed down, and hid. The second rabbit leaped up and repeated the process. Each rabbit in turn took over at the appropriate time, leaving the last rabbit to make a clean getaway.

I could almost hear each rabbit snickering behind the bushes. *"Heh, heh, heh. I can hardly wait for my turn. They'll eat my dust as I show those dogs my speed."*

All my life it seems as though I've been in pursuit of one type of rabbit after another. Just when I think my life is under control, something else leaps to the front and distracts me, leaving me to be always in the chase but never quite getting ahead. By watching the dogs, I learned to keep my eyes on my target. When it stops to rest, I also need to take a moment and regain my strength. Then I'll be ready to run again and have fun. I don't have to catch anything today. Tomorrow will be a new day, and there will always be more rabbits.

Even when I was scared, I could whistle and laugh, but I learned to respect the fears of others. Often I've faced a storm, pretending to be brave, but all the while ready to turn and run.

Braving the Storm

Bravely I stood facing the storm, shaking my fists at the sky.
"I'm as angry as you are. Don't you dare make me cry!"
The storm roared out an answer, one I couldn't comprehend.
From the clouds lightning flashed. This storm was not my friend.
"You think that I'm afraid to hear your mighty roar.
Through the years I've gotten strong. You don't scare me anymore."
My courage was ebbing fast, and I knew I had lied.
"Dogs, I think the storm is growing stronger.
Let's go inside and hide."

Loud Noises and the Storm

Our two German shepherds were frequently on self-imposed duty protecting the children. They lay quietly by the door, watching cars and people pass by on the street. Occasionally their heads would turn as they focused on certain sounds. If the sounds were benign or familiar, the dogs would return to their at-ease position. If the noises were loud or unusual, they'd face the perceived threat. Their low throaty growls would gradually get louder until the problem was resolved. They appeared rough and tough and ready for any situation that arose.

They bravely faced anything that seemed afraid of them. They were protective when they understood the situation. They always challenged intruders that encroached upon their space. They protected their food bowls. They protected the humans in their family, especially the younger ones. But noise? How could they protect against noise or attack noise? They learned to accept certain noises that were familiar to them, but the loud noises that rattled the windows and shook the house were not to be trifled with.

There were major exceptions to their tolerance for noise. Although they had been trained to ignore gunshots while in protection mode, they were never quite ready for fireworks and firecrackers. The sudden splashes of light and sound when pops and bangs came from varying locations startled them into bolting and running for cover. They never learned to adjust to fireworks, regardless of whether the explosions were large or small. The dogs seemed to be on high alert on special holidays. Tense and irritable already, as soon as the first firecracker exploded, both dogs became nervous, shaking puppies.

Thunderstorms were another source of noise that could not be avoided. When those dazzling displays of lightning occurred with accompanying thunder, Rex and Cleo would crowd closer to me, content only if I touched their heads and patted them occasionally. When thunder shook the house and jolted them out of their comfort zone, they dashed for the bed and wedged themselves underneath.

One Fourth of July, the dogs were already jittery and upset when a supercell moved into our area. The combination of fireworks and thunder created a special situation. To ease the tension I sat with dogs and children, talking and singing. I was hoping that everything would quickly pass. However, in the midst of this very loud and powerful storm, the power went out. It was already after ten o'clock, so my wife and I hurriedly put the children to bed and retired for the night. We lay in bed talking about the events of the day, the children, and our plans for tomorrow.

While the storm raged outside, we were warm and safe inside. Suddenly lightning struck a tree outside, ripping it apart, and the resulting boom rattled the house. Almost immediately the dogs dove under the bed. Our bed rose several inches. My wife screamed, which frightened our children; panic-stricken, they dashed in and piled on top of the bed.

As my wife tried to slide off the bed and get everyone resettled, she turned to get up. A head met hers, made one big slurp, and dove underneath the bed again. She screamed even louder this time.

Thinking we were under attack by the elements, I grabbed the children and headed for the basement. Rex and Cleo chose this exact moment to escape their close quarters. They jumped on the bed and in the process knocked my wife to the floor. She screamed again and fainted.

I called Rex and Cleo, and they slunk down the steps and hid. I went to find my wife, concerned that she was badly injured. She wasn't in bed, and I didn't find her in the bedroom. I couldn't see her on the other side of the bed, sprawled on the floor next to the wall.

I stumbled from room to room, tripping over all the things left behind when the lights went out, ignoring the pain as I continued to search. It seemed like an eternity before the lights flickered back on. The children climbed out of the basement, and I insisted they go back to bed. The dogs returned, and I sternly ordered them back to their beds, though they returned several times to see if I really meant for them to get out.

Although everything appeared to be returning to normal, I still hadn't found my wife. My mind was racing with possibilities, most of them bad. Had she ventured out into the storm? Was she injured or worse? My mind was exploding with possibilities.

Despite my commands, Rex and Cleo bounded past me and squeezed between the bed and the wall. Unfortunately, it was at that precise time that my wife awoke. She screamed again. The children heard her and came running, the dogs started giving her doggie kisses, and I was relieved to see she was alive and well. Now I thought she was injured for sure.

After the dogs and children were resituated, I pulled my wife to her feet.

She looked at me crossly. "Don't you dare say anything," she snapped.

I turned around and walked out onto the front porch. I studied the clear sky and took a deep breath of fresh air. I tried not to smile, but I couldn't help it.

A short time later, my wife joined me. "Aren't you coming back to bed?"

"I'll be there in a few moments. The air is so clean and crisp after a storm, and I want to enjoy it."

She put her arm around me. "I want to hear your version of tonight's events before I go to sleep. I'll bet it's funny."

"Honey, it wasn't funny until I knew you were okay." Then I grinned. "That's all. It was a rough, scary night. One I'll remember."

She hugged me, and we went inside. I knew then that things were going to be all right.

Life is always offering challenges. It is up to me to accept or reject them.

My two black Labradors, Roxy and Pixie, loved to run. I couldn't keep up with them unless I put on my Rollerblades and let them pull me as they ran for several blocks. When their energy had dwindled, they went into training mode, and we could travel at a more leisurely pace. Those first blocks were scary, challenging, and exciting all at the same time. The following true story is an example of one of those daily exercise routines.

Throwing Caution to the Wind!

Don't ask me if I do anything exciting. Just walking my Labradors can be exciting. On a peaceful Sunday afternoon, I took them for a walk. Well, not just a walk. I noticed they were really anxious to go out, so I thought I would just wear them down and get some exercise at the same time. So what better way for me to exercise than to rollerblade while the Labs pulled me around the block, down the streets, and along the sidewalks? After they got tired, I could rollerblade as long as I wanted.

They were a little more hyperactive than I thought. The first six blocks were really exciting as they ran at a gallop, straining against their leashes, while I blithely pretended to be a skier behind a boat. They frothed at the mouth, enjoying the freedom of running.

The first three miles weren't bad, but I noticed not everyone was cheerful as two large dogs came bearing down on them, with me in tow. The lady with the baby stroller and the small child didn't quit screaming until we were out of sight, but I suppose she was an exception. Most people didn't react quite that severely. I also admit to a little fear when we crossed the intersections at full speed, dodging and swerving past the oncoming cars. But my senses soon became numbed by overload. All was quite fine as I hung on, and I began to relax and enjoy the scenery. That is at least until *the cat.*

A cat lay on the sidewalk, dreaming of a faraway mouse, absorbing heat from the cement, seemingly unaware of impending disaster. Now at full speed, behind two already worn-out dogs, I thought I should be able to order them to stop, slow down, and heed my passionate pleas because, after all, I had once trained dogs, and I was thoroughly confident of my skills. Now as I look back at the situation, I realize my overconfidence was poorly misguided.

The sudden surge of power and speed was exhilarating as I shouted to the dogs to stop, slow down, and everything else I was calmly yelling at the time.

At that moment the cat awoke from his dream, recognized the impending peril from the approaching runaway team of dogs, and dashed across the street. The dogs followed suit, turning crisply ninety degrees in pursuit of the cat. At this point I kind of lost track of what happened because the dogs and I parted company.

As I flew through the air, I twisted and turned, trying to avoid the tree, the sidewalk, the street pavement, and other obstacles that suddenly flashed before me. Fortunately, I missed all but a bush and landed on some fairly soft earth. I released my hold on the dogs because they had already shifted into a higher gear.

The rest of the story was relatively uneventful because the cat had already planned his escape route. Dashing between two houses, he seemed to disappear.

Although the cat thought he was hidden, I saw where he had gone. While the two dogs ran excitedly around, the cat stretched out on a branch of a nearby tree, watching and smiling.

It took fifteen minutes of calling, pleading, and threatening to get the dogs back. They were having too much fun to listen to me.

After that, I was a bit sore, but wiser. Next time I would try to anticipate dangers and be ready to react should something unexpected occur. I thought it over all that night and decided that walking one dog at a time, without being on Rollerblades, would be best. But then again, how much fun would that be?

Throw caution to the wind! That's why I'll put on my Rollerblades for our next walk. Life is too short to worry about things like that.

Love between a dog and a person is rarely by chance. My experience is that it happens at first glance. There doesn't have to be bright lights and glitter. Suddenly you'll find you're the pick of the litter.

My Pick

You were my pick of the litter.
I didn't care that one of your eyes was blue
And the other one was gray.
It didn't matter that your coat was coarse
And the other pups were smooth and sleek.
One of your ears flopped down,
And the other stood straight and tall.
You were so cute dancing around your pen.
You were brave and fearless
As you faced the crowd.
But what I liked most of all
Was that you picked me.
You ignored the other kids and grown-ups.
You came over and licked my hand.
That was how I knew we were meant to be together.

A two-for-one special doesn't happen very often, and sometimes it's too much.

A Pet Store Special Deal

I was in the pet store, just looking around when I noticed two Labrador puppies trying to escape from their glass enclosure. A woman stopped to talk to them. One of the puppies came forward, demanding attention. The puppy was friendly and confident. The second puppy stayed out of reach, suspicious and unwilling to be touched. The woman moved on, but by then I was interested. *How will they react to me?* I wondered. I thought I should take a look at them also.

The sign on the enclosure said the female pups were from the same litter. I looked at them again. One pup had beautiful features while the other pup appeared to be more roughly hewn.

I need a dog, I told myself. *I'll look for the friendly one, the cute one, the most intelligent one, and the one with the best temperament.*

As I interacted with the two Labs, one dog displayed all the qualities I was looking for. She became my favorite, and soon I was at the counter ready to make my purchase. *One dog, forty dollars. One bag of dog food, twenty dollars. One leash, eight dollars. One harness, twenty dollars. One collar, five dollars.* I still had a few more items, and the total was already over ninety dollars. I gulped. This was more than I expected. After putting all the items back, I took one last look at my favorite. The initial cost was too much. Having a dog was not meant to be.

The person at the counter was not smiling anymore. "Sir, how about two dogs for the same price?"

I hesitated. There was something wrong with this picture.

"How about both dogs for free?"

I was in shock, so I said nothing. My head was spinning. *What is the catch?* I needed time to think this over. I started out the door.

"Okay, how about both dogs, two bags of dog food, two leashes, and two sets of the items you picked out, for free?" The store manager was not selling the dogs anymore but was pleading for me to take them.

"I've got to get these dogs out of here tonight. Last night they got out and wandered around the store, tearing things up, spooking the other animals, breaking things, and setting off the alarm. I need both of these dogs out of here tonight. I want them to go with someone or one or both of them will have to be put down."

I only wanted one dog, but I didn't want the other dog euthanized. I didn't want someone to be mean to the remaining dog either. I knew I would take care of them better than others could. "Okay, I'll take both of them."

Was I out of my mind? What would I do with two dogs? I tried to keep thinking that I got a great deal. I now had two dogs, two bags of food, two leashes, plus a few more doggie items. I knew I had my work cut out for me, but it was too late to say no.

Some people come into my life in unexpected ways. I'll learn to appreciate them and show love and kindness every day.

German shepherds that are trained take their protection roles very seriously. No intruders are allowed, and Santa is no exception.

Santa's Surprise

'Twas the night before Christmas and all across the yard,
Not a creature dared stir with German shepherds on guard.
My wife and children were in bed, secure in their sleep.
All dreams were about Christmas, no worries too deep.

Presents were wrapped and scattered around the tree.
The gifts were for the children, Emma, and me.
I had walked the dogs several blocks or more.
They were calmer now, so I hung their leashes by the door.

I was sitting at my computer, for I had poems to write,
When I heard a few growls, a snap, and a bite.
Two German shepherds had been my only alarm.
Someone had entered, perhaps with intent to harm.

I grabbed a leash and raced to the tree,
Wondering what kind of scene awaited me.
A red-suited man stood with his back to the wall.
He made no moves while the shepherds awaited my call.

The seat of his pants had been torn by a bite;
It would be a bit drafty the rest of the night.
"Your dogs are vicious. They bit, and I'll sue."
He sputtered obscenities until his face turned blue.

His demeanor was outrageous, considering his plight.
The dogs had him trapped. This would be a fun night.
"It seems to me you've invaded my space.
I've a right to protect my family and place.

"Since you come and go as if it doesn't matter,
This time you're wrong, for I'm a mad hatter."
His eyes grew wider as he studied my face.
"Perhaps my remarks were a bit out of place.

"I've got places to go and people to see.
Would you call off the dogs and let me be?
I'm a little tense from traveling all night.
I apologize for my temper. I'll make things right."

With one signal, I released the dogs from patrol.
They romped around Santa, though under control.
He gave each dog some chews and a bag full of toys.
Then he skipped around the tree without any noise.

Stockings were filled with all kinds of games,
Carefully marked with everyone's names.
Then up the chimney he rose in a hurry,
For outside the weather had turned to snow flurries.

I praised the dogs lavishly for guarding the house well.
No intruders could enter without encountering hell.
I slipped back to bed without writing a bit.
I didn't tell Emma because she wouldn't believe it.

"Now Brutus, now Killer, now Ty and Wolf,
Each one to your posts and guard the roof.
Santa might come back and give it another try.
Watch out for invaders that either walk or fly."

I was lying in bed with Emma at my side,
Still thinking of my dogs and beaming with pride,
When Emma quietly said, "Merry Christmas and good night.
Did you put the lid down and turn out the light?"

You'd think I'd remember each routine little task,
Just once without her having to ask.
The dogs were now restless, and there was no need to talk.
I knew it was late, but the dogs wanted to walk.

Some stories have a moral. I'll remember them.

Sirius, commonly called the Dog Star, is the brightest star in the sky and can be easily seen on winter and spring evenings. Sirius is part of the constellation Canis Major (Greater Dog). Ancient Egyptians thought heat from the Dog Star made the summer hotter. From that belief comes the expression, "the dog days of summer."

The Old Elephant and Sirius

Dust rose into the air as the old elephant shuffled along.
With every step she sang a traditional song,
A song she'd heard long ago as an elephant child,
A song she hadn't thought about in quite a while.

"As I travel on my way, I'll chant every word.
I'm too old to stay with the elephant herd.
The elephant graveyard will be my resting place.
No more lions or crocodiles will I face.

"Death is close. I can feel it in my bones.
I must remember the placement of the stones.
Thousands of my ancestors have come this way.
I must join them, perhaps this very day."

A gruff voice interrupted the elephant's reverie.
"Where are you going? You can walk with me."
She had not noticed the wild dog loping at her side.
He asked, "Do you need a friend in whom you can confide?"

He'd heard elephants went somewhere when they were old or sick.
He was sly, that wild dog, and he thought of a trick.
"I only want to help you," he said. "Don't get me wrong.
But didn't I just hear you chanting a song?"

Gently he urged, "Your destination, perhaps you'd like to share."
"If I told you I'd have to stomp you," she said with an angry stare.
He knew she was old, and he lost his sense of fear.
But he made a mistake when he thought she couldn't hear.

He mused aloud, "I know why she's walking here all alone.
If I follow her, I could discover a lot of precious bones.
A veritable treasure trove I might share with my pack.
They'd have a lifetime supply. No bones would they lack."

She listened carefully as he made his evil plan.
He didn't care if it was the elephants' sacred land.
By then she'd heard enough from that greedy dog.
She hurled him far, like a tiny log.

Some say he never returned and neither did he die.
Some say he watches way up in the sky.
They call him Sirius, the dog that once took flight.
Sirius, the Dog Star, the brightest star at night.

If I choose the right friends, they will tell me the truth, share slices of life, and listen.

Moses and George

It was evident in his bloodlines
When Moses was a young hound.
He was already the best tracker
If something needed to be found.

His nose was insured by Lloyds of London,
Which was a guarantee that his nose would not fail.
So when the circus lost an elephant,
They hired Moses, and he was soon on the trail.

Now an elephant is really hard to lose.
There's no place to hide one with ease.
But George was an unusual elephant.
He had learned to hide in the trees.

Moses started in the main ring of the big top,
The very last place George had been seen.
He definitely caught George's scent.
George needed a bath or two, if you know what I mean.

Moses may have been sidetracked
By all the circus sounds and smells,
For he lost George's scent right away.
It took him a while to pick up the trail.

George had not been kidnapped.
He wanted to leisurely bathe.
A swimming pool was too public.
He would have preferred a hidden cave.

Moses found George in the river,
Submerged and swimming around.
George looked surprised to see Moses.
"I'm not ready yet to be found!"

Moses agreed. Sometimes it's good to be alone.
It was hot that day and just right for a swim.
Moses went upstream a few yards
Before deciding to jump in.

George confided that he was tired of circus life,
Long days of working and getting up at dawn.
Moses listened to George's plight.
He was courteous. Not once did he yawn.

Moses and George became friends the moment they met.
Adventure called, and their destiny was set.
They didn't play the same kind of games,
But they could be friends just the same.

Hide and seek didn't give George a thrill.
Moses wouldn't play squish.
They sat and talked sometimes
And got in a game of Fish.

They were both happy to find the perfect friend.
Someone who would listen and was willing to share.
They formed a detective agency called
G-&-M Detective Agency, The Ones Who Care.

They're putting their talents together.
How well they'll do, who knows?
But they expect to solve a lot of cases
Because one has a great memory and the other has a great nose.

Friendship and love are works in progress. I can't reach higher levels or deeper understandings unless I'm willing to do whatever it takes.

The two friends in the following poem were all wrong for each other as far as size was concerned. One was a Great Dane and the other a Lhasa Apso. The size difference was neutralized because the Great Dane would lie down to play, and though he had great strength, he was gentle.

Two Friends

It's amazing how they look and turn
When they spot each other from afar.
How interested they are
To share all that they have learned.
They are friends, like Jeff and Mutt,
But size does not matter.
They ignore taunts or cutting remarks.
Their friendship will not tatter.
Through hard times or good,
They'll challenge the world.
Knowing what they've withstood,
Seeing their dreams unfurled,
To the end they'll face what comes.
Their friendship will cross the years.
They'll march to their own distant drums,
Ready for new frontiers.

We don't all have to see things the same way. I learn broader truths when I try to understand your point of view.

Point of View

Sometimes social correctness can be just a little tricky and all our best efforts can be for naught. We get caught up in looking at a problem from only one point of view. For example, there was the afternoon when my sister, Aubrey, went to visit Mom.

Aubrey pulled up into the driveway and got out of her car. A small dog ran up to Aubrey, sniffed, and stood beside her. She reached down and patted the dog. Just then Mom opened the door, greeted her, and invited her in.

The dog ran inside and through the open door as Aubrey entered. Mom grimaced but said nothing. They talked about small things and finally got around to discussing quilting.

The dog, meanwhile, was going in and out of the room, jumping up on furniture, and being a nuisance. Mom showed Aubrey some quilt pieces, and the dog grabbed one and ran.

Mom looked at Aubrey quizzically and said, "That dog is out of control!" But they patiently continued their conversation.

The dog demanded attention, barking, running in and out of the room, and coming back to nip at their hands, feet, and quilt pieces.

Aubrey politely petted the dog again until it jumped up into her lap. She shoved it down roughly and pushed it away. At that time Aubrey looked at Mom and stated, "Mom, I thought you said you would never get another dog again. Why did you change your mind?"

Mom looked surprised and exclaimed, "My dog! I thought that was your dog!"

Neither Mom nor Aubrey had communicated about the dog. Aubrey did not want to hurt Mom's feelings by telling her the dog was a nuisance. Mom, on the other hand, did not want to tell Aubrey the dog was not allowed in the house, not allowed to run around, and not allowed to chew on anything. As a consequence both became irritated, but they learned a valuable lesson.

Social correctness was very important to both of them. To say the wrong thing might have hurt their relationship because a tongue can be sharper than a sword. Both chose this time to be silent and look wise.

Later that day, both were laughing because they knew they had been fooled by the small dog. When Mom let it outside, it ran off, and she never saw it again. Her story was fun, but I wonder sometimes what the small dog told his friends.

Sad memories should be shared when silence becomes too loud.

Run Where the Flowers Grow

I couldn't believe my eyes.
Dad had brought home a surprise,
A black and white cocker spaniel.
She was a puppy, but she meant the world to me.
She was happy, playful, and made me smile.
Lady came when I called her, eager to please.
We were two friends, always at ease.
The two of us discovered the world anew.
Bonded by our hearts, our friendship grew.
We sniffed flowers. We chased birds.
I read stories, and she listened to every word.
When she was two, she followed me down
The dirt roads to the grocery store in our town.
We encountered few cars that hot summer day.
We crossed a two-lane county road on our way.
Before I got groceries, the owner and I had a debate.
But he said, "No dogs allowed. She'll have to wait."
When I looked for her, she had crossed the street.
She was busy sniffing flowers or looking for bugs to eat.
My first thought was, *She shouldn't be over there.*
Without thinking, I whistled, loud and clear.
The shrill sound hung expectantly in the air.
It was then that I saw a speeding car
And realized that it wasn't very far.
At the same time I saw Lady raise her head,
And obediently toward me she sped,
Smiling with every stride.
"Stop, Lady! Stop!" I wish I'd cried.
But I was frozen, watching this nightmarish scene:
The car and Lady and the gap closing in between.

There was a loud *whump!*
Time stopped, and I had no need for air.
The car had hit Lady, and the driver seemed unaware.
He slowed and then sped up. I knew he didn't care.
I ran to her and dropped to my knees.
"Lady, get up! I'm sorry. Please."
I held her lifeless form tight,
Wishing with all my might
That this was just a bad dream in the night.
I walked home in a trance,
Angry at myself for what I had done.
Why had I whistled without a glance?
Why had I done this to my friend?
Blaming myself over and over again.
Tears streaming down my face,
I somehow managed to carry her to our place.
Mom took the groceries,
And told me to hold Lady for a few minutes more,
And I did until I collapsed spiritless on the floor.
The next day we held a private ceremony with a prayer.
Only family was invited there.
My heart pounded, and my head hurt.
With each shovelful of dirt,
I thought I could hear a whistle blow.
Before I left, I leaned down and whispered softly,
"Run, Lady. Run where the flowers grow."

We'll grow together through adversity and be loyal to the end.

The Stray

I asked my neighbor about his dog,
Because she kept him always within her sight.
He said slowly, "She showed up one day."
He paused. "Someone didn't treat her right."

She seemed affectionate, loyal, and smart.
He reached down and scratched her behind the ears.
"She was starving, scared, and half out of her mind."
As he spoke, his eyes filled up with tears.

"She was scrawny and malnourished
When I first saw her slinking over the hill.
She would sneak up and gulp down any scraps
Left by dog or cat until she had her fill.

"I yelled at her the first three days,
Emphatically telling her to go back home.
'Stay at your own house.
Don't come over here to roam!'

"But I got to noticing how poorly she looked
While she was inhaling the food in gulps.
Then I watched how she always hurried away.
I knew right then she had pups.

"I tried to follow her home one day,
But she was determined to give me the slip.
I lost her trail in the snowy woods.
For me, it was a wasted trip.

"I began giving her five cans of food each day,
Just until the start of spring.
Then one morning she didn't show up.
I thought it was the end of everything.

"In the late afternoon she appeared again,
Carrying something I couldn't quite see.
At first she wouldn't let me get close to her.
She didn't trust anyone, and that included me.

"Yet her hunger brought her near,
And I saw what she protected so well.
It was a pup she toted around with her,
But it was dead. It was easy to tell.

"For several days she carried that pup,
Though by then it was only a hide.
But the mom refused to release her grip.
She had a burning love inside.

"Finally she laid her pup down,
Close to the northern fence.
She joined up with my other two dogs,
And she's been here since.

"I don't know where she came from.
I don't know where she's been.
But I do know she guards the place,
And I consider her my friend."

With a nod and that explanation he strode away,
The dog right there by his side.
I was left with a lump in my throat
But a warm feeling deep inside.

If I want to be treated like a prince, I should act like a prince and treat others royally.

The Princess and the Wannabe (Or the Lhasa Apso and the Chihuahua)

The wannabe hates you to compare
Her with the princess.
(Don't you even dare.)
She's jealous and thinks she's just as fair.
She wants to be pretty too.
But she doesn't have the attitude
To make her dreams come true.
She's grouchy in the morning,
And usually the rest of the day.
Yet she wants all the attention
To be directed her way.
She has a snarl on her face
And wonders why strangers avoid her
Or give her lots of space.

The princess is pretty, kind, and sweet,
Delicate and choosy, tomboyish, and neat.
She also expects attention, yet she enjoys being alone.
She's content in a garden or sitting on a throne.
Smiles are for everyone, whether pauper or king.
She loves everybody and enjoys everything.
Sensitive and caring, she listens when you sigh.
Her heart is tender. She doesn't want you to cry.
Everybody is her very best friend.
They'll agree with that too.
Once you've looked into her eyes,
Her love comes shining through.

The princess and the wannabe,
How can I compare the two?
They're as different as different can be.
That's what I would tell you.
Each one has a beautiful face.
Each is loved by her mother.
Each one has her own space,
And each is devoted to the other.
But even so, as jealousy goes
Their bond is very thin.
Someday they might be foes
If something snaps within.
But for now it's grins and smiles.
Love is shared all around.
You might go thousands of miles
Before stronger ties are found.

A good friend listens and is willing to help.

Bonnie and Clyde

"Please come get your dog! She's trying to attack my dog!" Someone was pounding on my door, ringing my doorbell, and calling my name. My neighbor stood there wringing her hands. "Please come get your dog!" she pleaded again.

I had been a dog foster parent for two weeks, and I had posted pictures of these beautiful dogs on the Internet. I was waiting for German shepherd lovers to speak up and adopt Bonnie and Clyde, but no one appeared to be willing. Now Bonnie was terrorizing the neighborhood, and I was shocked. She seemed okay with grown-ups, and she adored children, but I soon found out she didn't like small dogs or cats.

The two German shepherds were living with me in the house at night but staying in my garage during the day. Now on two consecutive days Bonnie had escaped the confines of the garage and roamed the neighborhood. I thought she might have to be put down if I couldn't find an immediate solution. How was she getting out? Had I been so careless as to leave the garage door up?

Bonnie enjoyed running around outside and would slip back home before I found her missing. She was very smart, but her obedience training needed to be tweaked a little. My neighbor insisted that Bonnie should be caught in the act of escaping. She was probably getting help.

The other German shepherd was two years old, very loving, and a little bit dopey. He didn't seem to be involved, but I believed my neighbor was right. There had to be some way to find out what was going on.

Although the dogs knew I sometimes waited in the car, they paid me no attention. Their lives returned to their normal routines. For the next three days Bonnie did nothing suspicious. On the fourth day she started whining. Clyde got up off his bed and stood by Bonnie. She whined again. Clyde walked across the garage floor, stood up on his back legs, and deliberately hit the keypad, which was six feet high. The garage door rolled up, and she walked out, ready for another day of fun.

"Not so fast, Bonnie," I stated. *"Komm! Hier!"* She was stunned to hear a command in German. She turned and came right to me. *"Platz!"* She lay down. *"Blieb!"* From then on she got commands in German, and we reviewed what she needed to do. Clyde, on the other hand, only understood English. And he understood Bonnie's need for escape.

It was inconvenient for me but I locked the garage doors. The dogs had to know that their behavior was unacceptable and that commands given were meant to be followed. For the next two weeks I was strict, and they listened and thrived. By the time new owners were found and accepted, I had grown fond of Bonnie and Clyde. But I had done my job for the moment, and when the next foster home was needed, I was ready.

Some dogs we select to become part of our families. Other times, the dogs join our families through circumstances beyond our control. In either case, once dogs touch our hearts, they are part of our families forever.

Tripod, the Miracle Dog

"Tripod?" many people said. "That's a funny name for a dog. Why did you call her that?"

It was a question that brought memories of a cold and stormy evening. My wife and I were alone when the phone rang. Something was wrong. I could hear the anguish in my son's voice as he mumbled again.

I asked, "Have you been in an accident? Who's hurt and bleeding?"

My son repeated his message more clearly this time. "We found a dog. Can we bring her home?" He explained how he and his friend had stopped at the neighborhood park. They had seen an animal curled up, lying by a table. They hadn't been sure if it was dead or alive, so they took a closer look.

They decided it was a Boston terrier, bloody, wet, and shivering, with teeth that had been kicked out and one leg hanging uselessly by its side. It was barely breathing and had a weak pulse. He was sure the dog would die within a few hours.

"Can I bring her home?" His voice was soft and pleading. How could I possibly say no to a dog in that condition? And how could I say no to him for doing a good deed?

We already had three dogs, but we could care for the dog at least for the evening. If she survived the evening, we would decide what to do with her in the morning.

Later when my daughter arrived home from work, she began crying when she saw this mistreated little dog. The dog's large brown eyes seemed to say, *I'm helpless and wounded. Would you help me?*

Shocked by the dog's condition, she took charge. She found a box, put some towels in it, and loosely wrapped a blanket around the shivering dog. She brought the box into the living room, placed it in front of the fireplace, and slept at the dog's side. She was determined to keep the dog warm throughout the night.

The next morning the terrier was trembling and weak but still alive. I took the dog to the vet and explained the condition we found her in. He confirmed our suspicions. Somebody had taken out his aggression on this dog, breaking her hind leg and knocking out most of her teeth. The vet gave her a shot and antibiotics but didn't think she would make it another day.

With my daughter's care, Tripod squeezed out another day and then a week, and finally she was up and skipping about, dragging that useless leg behind her. My son had already named her Tripod because she balanced on three legs. Our other three dogs, two Labs and a basset hound, treated her with respect and gentleness, sensing her fragile condition.

Tripod was the most affectionate dog I had ever known, always smiling and glad to be alive. She was also happy to have food and shelter and, of course, love.

Over the next year she gradually filled out and gained confidence. One morning Tripod surprised us with a new miracle. While we were on one of our long walks, she ran with the other dogs, testing her once useless leg. Within a week she regained most of the use of her hind leg. She was a tripod no longer, but the name stuck.

Every dog has a role in life. Knowing what is expected gives that dog a chance to relax and enjoy life.

Scooter

Scooter had already established bad habits when I entered the family. She went where she wanted, did not respond to basic obedience commands, and nipped anyone who invaded her space. Much of her behavior needed to be changed.

I didn't appreciate her growling at me or nipping me when I put on her leash for walking. I expected her to stay by my side and follow directions. I didn't want her wandering into the road or chasing butterflies.

We had our little "talks." I would carefully explain how things had changed and she would cooperate or else. Then we would go on little walks, and we practiced walking and turning together. After a couple of sessions she eyed me suspiciously but reluctantly acknowledged that I was in charge.

I soon realized we would have to compromise. Even though she tried to keep up with me, her nose proved to be a problem. She was easily sidetracked by bugs, flowers, and other fascinating things. Off she would go, straining at her leash, tracking a new scent. Scooter would never be like the other dogs. She was a purebred basset hound, and tracking animals and scents was part of her heritage. I eased up on making her follow directions but insisted that she be courteous.

The Labs had to teach Scooter another lesson. Scooter guarded every bowl of food savagely. She would growl and snap, nipping at the two larger dogs. She didn't seem to realize that they stayed away because I watched them closely.

One day Pixie had enough of Scooter's aggressiveness. I was distracted and on the phone. When Pixie came too close to Scooter's food dish, Scooter snapped at Pixie and drew blood. Drops of blood dripped from Pixie's nose.

Before I could stop Pixie, Scooter was on the floor, her neck exposed, and she was pleading for mercy. I dashed over, thinking Pixie had Scooter in a death grip. When I yelled, Pixie reluctantly backed away, letting Scooter scramble to her feet and regain her composure. I checked her over and declared she wasn't really hurt. Of course Scooter was bruised and scared. But now she knew her reign was over. From then on when Roxy and Pixie were at their food dishes, Scooter made a wide circle around them to get to her bowl. She didn't challenge the bigger dogs again.

Because there were four dogs in my house, I had to pay close attention when children were visiting. The children would look at my Labs, Roxy and Pixie, and decide they were too big and scary. But in fact, the Labs adored children and were very gentle. Tripod was fragile and timid, and the children would leave her alone. The children would invariably make a beeline to Scooter, the dog that appeared to be cuddly. She would try to slip away but she was always trapped. Scooter was not as friendly as basset hounds are supposed to be. She would snap and nip and make the kids cry.

Scooter's nose worked overtime. She followed her nose everywhere. When she was on the trail of an animal or food, she was focused and could not always be persuaded to leave the scent. Usually she was not aware of other things happening around her. I thought her ability for tracking was wasted, but one day she proved me wrong.

That day was simply gorgeous. Sunshine splashed over everything, and I wanted to stay home and soak it in. The morning was perfect, and I sang along with the car radio as I headed to work. There was nothing in the local news that sparked my interest, but I listened to the weatherman talk about the possibility of a thunderstorm with hail. My car would be outside and could be damaged.

I kept a wary eye on the sky, but it remained clear. On my way home later that day, I noticed a storm approaching from the west; ominous clouds towered high. Occasional streaks of lightning emphasized the need for me to go straight home and get my car in the garage. As I turned into my neighborhood, the sky had turned an eerie greenish white.

I pulled my car into the garage just as the downpour started. In the house, I went from room to room, but no one was home except for the dogs. Two loud claps of thunder shook the house before hail began bouncing off the ground and pounding on the roof. The dogs crawled under beds, trying to escape the scary sounds. I called them, and we went into the basement, where it was quieter. The neighborhood siren went off. Tornado! I cowered in a corner with the dogs. There was a brief silence. A roar began nearby and grew closer. Then silence again.

"I guess it missed us," I said to the dogs.

I went outside and saw several houses had been damaged. Farther up the hill, some homes had been flattened, and people were frantically searching through the debris. I leashed the Labs and Scooter and went to help. That's when I learned Scooter's real value.

While I kept the two Labs with me, one searcher took Scooter. With her acute sense of smell, she quickly located two people trapped under some of the wreckage, and then she eagerly continued searching. For the first time I really appreciated her for what she could do. She had earned a measure of respect from me. In turn, she became a more contented dog, happy to have found her own role.

Everything is worth a good sniff. I'll sniff the air after a good rain, listen to the meadowlarks singing, count the dew drops on a rose, and taste ripe strawberries. But I think a smell brings back the best memories.

Life is too short to worry about consequences. If you boldly take action, you can sometimes drive your troubles away.

Sammy, the Self-Appointed Neighborhood Watchdog

Snow had fallen in the early morning hours and was lying crisp and pristine on the streets and lawns. Those who went to work early relied on their four-wheel drives to get them to the main road. Mothers trying to get their children to the bus stops and people who had places to go waited for the snowplow to come. I stood at the window, drinking coffee and debating whether to shovel the snow off my driveway or wait until later.

At this time, Sammy, a well-fed golden retriever, emerged from his warm house, eager to see what new and exciting things were happening in the world. There were no deer or other animals to chase away. Everything was under control. Then he spotted the snowplow coming down the hill. The snowplow was roaring and throwing snow high into the air and off to the side.

As I watched Sammy, I could guess what he was thinking. He was shocked to see a new menace advancing down the road. The invader was attacking the street and destroying the peaceful neighborhood. This was more than he could take.

Sammy dashed about, barking and leaping. The snowplow driver, distracted momentarily, pulled over to the side. Up the hill, a family preparing for school heard the commotion and came out to watch the action. A woman farther up, impatient and seeing that the snowplow had stopped, decided to venture out on her own. Her car's tires slid and spun, slid and spun, as she lost traction and control on the icy street. Her efforts to go forward were useless. The harder she tried, the worse it became. Gradually she slid backward down to the cul-de-sac at the bottom of the street and stopped in front of the snowplow.

I pulled up a chair and waited to see what would ensue. A pickup carefully came down the hill, and soon the car was hooked up and towed.

During this time Sammy stood and watched, breathing heavily from all the exercise, and waited for the monster to continue. When the snowplow went back to work, Sammy returned to his protective mode, barking and leaping. When the snowplow was finally out of sight, Sammy, the self-appointed neighborhood watchdog, collapsed on the road.

Convinced he had driven off the evil, horrible invader, Sammy went back to his driveway and took a long-deserved nap.

Beowulf

Beowulf, my German shepherd, taught me a lot about life. First, someone has to be in charge. Dogs are pack animals and need structure in their lives. Second, the leader has to be consistent, or order breaks down and all things that have been learned previously will start unwinding. Third, praise and love are far more important than criticism. These rules apply well to dogs, but they also work well with most people.

When I got Beowulf, he was two months old, all cuddly and very much a puppy. He was small, but his large paws told me he would grow much larger. His ears flopped over. He ambled clumsily over and licked my hand.

My girlfriend was watching. "He's adorable. You just have to buy him."

I lived in an apartment, and I was still in college. I was not ready to take on the responsibilities of raising a puppy. Neither did I have a place for the puppy to play and exercise. In spite of the reasons I had for not getting a puppy, I couldn't resist and got him anyway.

I knew when to take Wulf, his name was shortened by then, outside. I rushed him outside after he ate, drank water, got up from sleep, before he went to sleep, and anytime he appeared restless or was looking around for a spot. In other words, I took him outside frequently. Gradually he learned to wait by the door. During the day while I attended classes, there were occasional stains. It wasn't his fault. I knew he would rather go outside. Dogs don't like to soil their living spaces.

As he went through the teething stage, a new problem developed. While I was gone, Wulf would chew anything within his reach. Corners of books, electrical cords, and furniture—all were fair game. Finally, I began putting him in a crate with things he was allowed to gnaw on. This was for his safety, my peace of mind, and for learning how to travel.

I had to learn to be consistent with his training. When he was six months old, I took him to beginning obedience classes. I soon learned that I was the one being trained. He needed me to be the leader of his pack.

After I learned my role, Wulf learned to follow directions extremely well. Every day, morning and evening, we practiced fifteen minutes going through our drills before going for a walk. He could sit, lie down, walk by my side at any pace I chose, and stay. Both of us became conditioned mentally as well as physically.

Not only in the early stages of training but whenever Wulf followed directions I was quick to pat his chest and give him praise. He learned English and German voice commands as well as hand signals. We took advanced training, and the workouts became more intense. I didn't need to go to the gym during this time. I was getting enough exercise.

We proceeded through protection training. He learned to protect on command and to relax on command. His training included mastering obstacle courses, climbing seven-foot barriers, and search and rescue. The more that was expected, the more Wulf responded. He was always well behaved, loveable, and very protective.

Wulf, like the other dogs trained for protection, was a family dog. It was never acceptable to growl at a family member. His role was to protect when needed and to love his family always.

Dogs won't be perfect all the time. They make mistakes sometimes even if they're well trained. But if their masters are in charge, are consistent, and give frequent praise, dogs are eager to please. They remember who cares for them, pets them, and gives them praise. Because of that, dogs show their love and become extremely loyal. Wulf was an example of a well-trained dog.

After a long day of work it's common for dog owners to rush home. They know their dogs are waiting for them, ready to greet them with dog kisses and love.

Best Friends

Dog, we played for hours
Under that tree,
Wrapped in the shade,
Just you and me.
Not one word was needed
Or carelessly said,
Just thoughts of how I was lucky
Within my head.
You were handed over to me
As a small pup.
Now you are my best friend,
All grown up.
Everywhere I go you give me joy.
I'll take you along.
You'll be right by my side,
Where you belong.
I don't know what we're gonna do
This coming year
When I go off to school.
We'll play it by ear.
I won't shed any tears.
Mom says I'll be a little man,
Marching out the gate.
You'll see the world while I'm gone,
But you'll have to wait.
I'll hurry home to see you, best friend.
I don't want to be late.

Dogs don't seem to worry about getting tricked. If they fall for some trick, they don't get embarrassed. They leave problems to their masters. They go about their routines as if nothing ever happened.

Watchdogs!

My brother had two white German shepherds. The male, the larger of the two, appeared to be the ideal watchdog. When Zip was sitting in the yard, he looked absolutely scary, and it seemed highly unlikely that an intruder would dare to challenge him. He looked and acted as though he could make short work of someone's leg bone. Even though I knew Zip, I didn't enter the yard without my brother present. There was no doubt Zip could handle almost any situation.

Zip had one weakness. Although protective, he wouldn't bite girls or women, especially little ones. He would growl and show his teeth at males, while females were not only safe around him but little girls were even protected.

Lady, the female German shepherd, was different. She was almost half the size of Zip, but she always meant business. She would bite any intruder, male or female, who entered the yard without a member of the family standing nearby. My brother and his wife were confident that the two dogs would keep everyone outside the fenced yard.

Josh, their son, had a girlfriend who attended the same high school as him and the same church as his family, and they had many friends in common. Often their activities were centered on things both Josh and Lisa liked to do. On Josh's birthday Lisa suggested that they all go to a pizza place downtown. That seemed like a good idea because Josh loved pizza, and his parents thought it would be a chance to become better acquainted with Lisa.

When they finished the pizza, they all sat for a while and talked. Lisa seemed to be having an especially good time. Conversation was easy because it was about school, church, and friends.

They took Lisa home, and her parents met them at the door. Her parents seemed embarrassed and apologetic. Lisa's father took a deep breath and said, "I'd like to show you a video the kids took while you were gone."

The video showed a group of kids putting rolls of toilet paper all over their house, in the trees, and even in the bushes. The kids were laughing and enjoying the joke they had pulled.

My brother and his wife sat there in stunned silence as they watched the kids toilet papering their home. They weren't sure what kind of reaction was expected. They were shocked that their watchdogs had not been there to bite or growl. They were left wondering why neither of the dogs appeared in the video.

Lisa's parents had the answer. They explained that Josh had given Lisa the clue that enabled the kids to pull off the caper. He had mentioned that the male dog would not hurt a girl or a woman and was even protective of a young girl.

The group had used that information to their advantage. What had once been a difficult problem had become easy. They had lowered Lisa's little sister over the fence. The male shepherd had gone into protective mode and placed himself between her and the female dog. With the male dog running interference the little girl enticed the dogs into the garage and locked the door.

The rest of the group had entered the yard and began decorating at leisure without worrying about the dogs. After their deed was done they had stood there and laughed, feeling secure that they had outwitted Josh and his parents.

As my brother and his family watched the activities taking place, they weren't amused. Their security system had failed right before their eyes.

Josh seemed unusually quiet and upset, and when they arrived home, he broke the silence. He claimed Lisa had betrayed their friendship. She had used information he had given her in confidence to pull a prank on his family. She had also lured the family away from the house, using his birthday as an excuse. She had been in on the plan right from the beginning. It seemed everyone but the family had been in on the joke.

The dogs weren't in trouble. Zip and Lady had only done what was expected. They went back to their routines of racing beside the fence and challenging any intruders. The family, however, decided to improve their security system. I'm not sure what they did because they kept that a secret. I do know they got another female shepherd. Zip couldn't keep both away at the same time.

That was also the end of a friendship. Josh and Lisa did not agree on the results of the prank. Lisa thought it was harmless and fun, while Josh thought it was a violation of trust and loyalty. Neither could understand the other's way of thinking.

Poor Charlee

Where is the dog that played all day?
She's lying stiff and silent in my doorway.
Just a few weeks ago she had life and fire,
A special kind of spirit that was hard to acquire.
Who poisoned this dog, I want to know.
She was a puppy and starting to grow.
Friendly and inquisitive, everyone was a friend.
Did someone really want her life to end?
What percentage of lives lost is considered okay?
How many pets have to suffer and pass away?
I thought I would love her until her dying breath.
What could I have done to prevent her death?

Since 2007 the American Veterinary Medical Association has issued
alerts regarding diseases similar to Fanconi syndrome in dogs. The
problem, a disorder of the kidney tubes, appeared to be connected
to the consumption of chicken jerky treats made in China. The FDA
was alerted to the rising number of pet fatalities, but the levels of
toxins and contaminants were not considered high enough to take
action.

Over the last eight years I've given chicken jerky treats to my
own dogs as rewards. The dogs responded well, and I thought the
quality of the chicken treats was exceptional. However, over the past
six months I began to see differences between packages.

Some of the treats were dry, and others seemed slightly moist,
but I continued to purchase the treats simply because the dogs
liked them and I had confidence in certain companies. I assumed
those companies would put their names only on quality products.

I thought my dogs, my friends, would be protected. I saw no warnings posted, and I had a false sense of security.

In late November, Charlee, my eight-month-old German shepherd, began showing strange symptoms. After eating she would throw up. Then came excessive drooling, lethargy, and a refusal to eat. In my own ignorance I gave her more chicken strips to keep her from starving. She would eat those but little else. Finally I took her to the veterinarian. In December, the veterinarian noted she had problems concerning her digestive system, but in his report he said her general condition was good. He said nothing about her kidneys failing. Charlee continued to suffer, and two days later, she was dead.

One month later I was in a large chain store. I headed toward the dog food section and made my selection. I dragged a large bag of dry dog food to my cart.

"Dog treats," I said aloud. "Now I'll get chicken strips."

The aisle was blocked. I noticed an employee busily taking packages of chicken strips off the shelves. She refused to let me take anything. "Everything that was made in China is being recalled. You can't buy any chicken strips or other treats."

When I returned home, I searched the Internet for news about the recall. I was shocked to see that the problem was noted as early as 2005, but several major companies ignored the warnings and waited until they were forced to take action.

Several kinds of dog food were finally being recalled. Poor Charlee. The recall came too late to save her life.

Dogs have always been part of my life. I've trained, raised, loved, and buried them. My heart has learned how to love unconditionally and to let go when they die. They have enriched my life and taught me to embrace the world with curiosity and abandon.

In my lifetime I have encountered angels and demons in many shapes and sizes. I have often been slow in evaluating people and their motives. During these times I've sometimes wished that I knew what dogs inherently know. I don't know which people are friends and which are foes. My dog knows, but I forget to ask.